Helpful Betty

to the rescue

For Tim—MK

For Belinda, who helped—MM

Helpful Betty

to the rescue

Story by Michaela Morgan
Illustrated by Moira Kemp

More than anything else,

Betty likes to be helpful.

One day,

while she is busy wallowing

with the other hippos,

she hears a cry...

"EEP! EEP!"

"It's just a monkey in a tree,"

says Arthur, the oldest hippo.

"Keep on wallowing."

But Betty springs

into action.

"A poor little monkey

stuck in a tree?

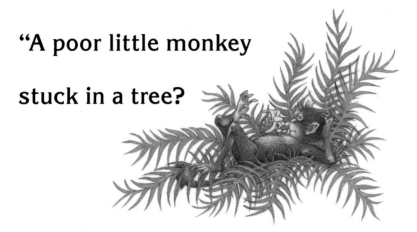

This is a job for helpful me!"

"But Betty," says Arthur,

"monkeys can . . ."

Too late—

Betty is off and running.

"Zippety zoom, zippety zee,

here comes super-speedy me,

leaping and flying

as fast as a flea," she sings,

until . . .

she runs out of breath.

But just then

she spots a short cut,

with stepping stones.

So over she steps.

"Trippety trip, skippety skee,

here comes super-helpful me,

leaping and flying

as fast as a flea,

tripping and skipping

delicately," she sings,

until . . .

she runs out

of stepping stones.

But just then

she spots

a floating log.

So on she springs.

"Fa-la-la, fiddle-dee-dee

here comes graceful little me,

leaping and flying

as fast as a flea,

light as a leaf floating free,"

she sings,

until . . .

her log snaps.

But just then

she spots a handy branch.

So off she springs.

"Alley-oop, one, two, three,

here comes acrobatic me,

leaping and flying

as fast as a flea,

tripping and skipping

delicately,

light as a leaf floating free,

flying and swinging

courageously," she sings,

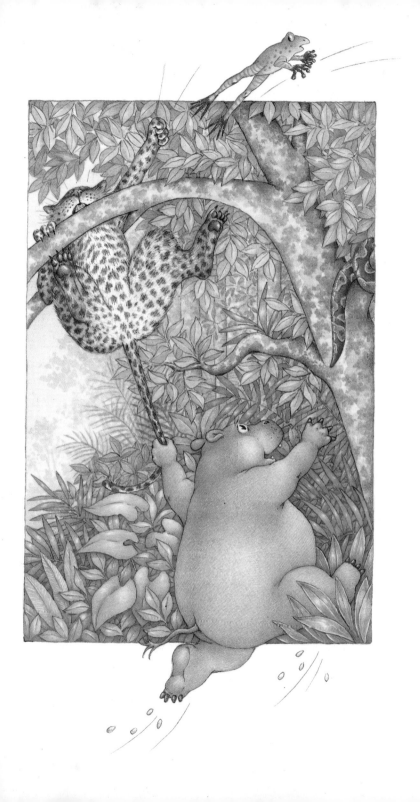

until . . .

her branch hisses,

and just then...

she lands.

"EEP!" cries the monkey.

"Poor little monkey,

stuck in a tree,

you are a job for helpful me!

I'm scrambling

and clambering

through the tree,

like a little monkey ...

oh!"

Betty has a thought.

"Yes," says the monkey,

"monkeys can

climb up trees."

"Aha," says Betty.

"They can climb down,

too," says the snake.

"Oh," says Betty.

"And hippos can't,"

says the leopard.

"AAGH!" cries Betty.

"So I can't rescue anything,"

she wails.

"Well," says the frog,

"you did rescue me,

but I don't think you noticed."

Betty is pleased.

"So I *am* a brave

and helpful hippo after all,"

she says.

"But now I'm just

a poor little hippo,

stuck in a tree."

"Not for long," says the frog.

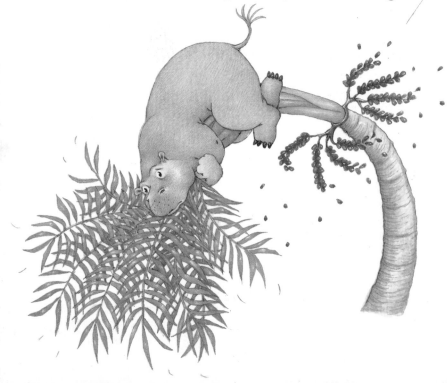

BOING! The tree springs up,

and SPLATT! Betty lands...

all ready to help someone else.

This edition first published 1994 by Carolrhoda Books, Inc.
Produced by Mathew Price Ltd, Old Rectory
House, Marston Magna, Yeovil, Somerset BA22 8DT, England

Carolrhoda Books, Inc. c/o The Lerner Group
241 First Avenue North, Minneapolis, MN 55401

Library of Congress Cataloging-in-Publication Data

Morgan, Michaela.
   Helpful Betty to the rescue / by Michaela Morgan ; illustrated by
Moira Kemp.
      p.   cm.
   Summary: Helpful Betty the hippopotamus hears a cry and sets off to
rescue a monkey she assumes is stuck up in a tree.
   ISBN 0-87614-831-3
   [1. Hippopotamus—Fiction.   2. Helpfulness—Fiction.]   I. Kemp,
Moira, ill.   II. Title.
PZ7.M8255He   1994
[E]— dc20   93-39885
                                                          CIP
                                                           AC

Printed in Hong Kong
Bound in the United States of America

1 2 3 4 5 6 – I/OS – 99 98 97 96 95 94